GLORY GATE

Written by Sally Odgers

Cover Illustration by Shawn Shea

CONTENTS

Chapter 1
WHITE SHIRTS AND LAVENDER HOUSES

"Why do wars begin?" the whiteshirt asked.

The whiteshirt was Gavven's new class teacher. The man had a real name, of course, but Gavven couldn't remember at the moment what it was. He couldn't remember a lot of things this week. He couldn't remember the names of any of the new teachers and he couldn't remember the new names they'd given to the subjects he was being taught. He couldn't remember the answer he was supposed to give to the question, either. But he knew it had an answer because all the questions did.

"It's a lot easier now," Gavven's friend Jamal was always saying. "You don't have to answer in your own words. You just answer the way the teacher tells you."

That was all very well for Jamal, but Gavven was good at putting things in his own words. He liked thinking about what he might say. He wasn't so good at remembering things he was told to say.

Jamal was different. Jamal always got all his multiplication tables right, every time, but when it came to writing a story, Jamal had trouble thinking of anything to write. Up until last week, Gavven had often helped Jamal with his work. Now it was Jamal who had to help Gavven.

"Why do wars begin?" the whiteshirt asked again. "Gavven? What is the answer?"

Gavven looked helplessly at the teacher. "I can't remember," he said.

The whiteshirt frowned slightly. "You should know the answer to this one, Gavven," he said. "You knew it yesterday."

Gavven slowly shook his head. He couldn't remember. "Is it because one country tries to take something that really belongs to another country?" he asked.

"No, Gavven," the whiteshirt said. "That isn't the answer. The answer is that wars begin because people are different."

"Oh," Gavven said. He remembered now, but he still didn't understand. What did it matter if people were different, as long as they were decent to one another?

"You will need to remember that," the whiteshirt said.

Gavven nodded. He would try to remember it, but he still didn't think it was right.

There were actually a lot of things that Gavven didn't think were right, but there was nothing he could do about them. Things were changing so quickly he hardly had time to blink!

Last semester, school was exactly like it had always been. Ms. Chang, who had taught Gavven all the way through the first half of the year, had been there. Ms. Chang liked multiplication tables and spelling. It always seemed a little silly to learn these when they all had a spellcheck and a mathcheck on their mini-computers, but Ms. Chang said it was important to know how things worked.

"When I was a little girl, back in 2000, we had to wait to use computers because we had only one computer per classroom," Ms. Chang used to tell them. "That meant we did a lot of work by writing with pens or pencils."

"Paper books?" Gavven asked.

"That's right. We used books or notebooks that were made of paper."

Jamal had laughed at that. So had some of the others. Imagine writing in books made of paper! That was so old-fashioned! But then, Ms. Chang was pretty old. She was older than most grandmothers.

"It's very important to think hard about your work," Ms. Chang said. "I can tell you that four groups of four equal sixteen. Your mathcheck will tell you that in an instant, but you won't really believe it until you learn it for yourselves."

Ms. Chang had given Gavven four blocks. Jamal had four blocks, as did Ember and Jamal's twin sister, Indiri. They put the four groups of four together and then counted to make sure there were sixteen. Of course there were, but now it made more sense. Four groups of four really were sixteen.

"You see?" Ms. Chang said. "You have proved it to yourselves. That's how important discoveries are made. People ask questions, then they find possible answers and try to prove whether they are right or wrong."

"What if nobody asked questions?" Indiri wanted to know.

Ms. Chang smiled at her. "If nobody asked questions, we would still believe the stars were holes in the sky. If nobody asked questions, we would still believe the earth was flat. If nobody asked questions, we would never have heard of Glory Gate."

Everyone groaned. They all were tired of hearing about Glory Gate – a gateway that led into other worlds. It had sounded so exciting when it was discovered, but it turned out that only astronauts and scientists were allowed to go through it. Gavven's dad worked at the Glory Gate Center, but he never said much about it at home. Especially since the center had been taken over by the government.

Gavven liked the way Ms. Chang taught things. He liked Ms. Chang, but suddenly, over the winter break, there had been a worldwide political election and everything had changed.

Ms. Chang and all the other teachers Gavven knew were suddenly gone and new teachers arrived. The new teachers all looked alike. They had brown hair and pale skin and they all wore tight white shirts. They all walked very stiffly, almost as if they were marching.

The new teachers weren't mean – in fact, they never got irritated. They patiently told students things over and over and over again until the students got them right. The trouble was, they never really explained anything so that Gavven could understand.

Now the whiteshirt looked at Gavven again. "Why do wars begin?" he asked.

This time, Gavven was ready. "Wars begin because people are different."

"Good!" the whiteshirt said. "What would be a good way to keep wars from beginning?"

Jamal raised his hand. "I know!"

"All right then, Jamal. You may answer the question," the whiteshirt said.

Jamal grinned from ear to ear. He was good at remembering, and he knew this one! "A good way to keep wars from beginning is to make people all the same."

"Very good, Jamal," the whiteshirt said. "Now, here's a harder question. What if people are not all the same? What can we do then?"

Jamal stopped smiling. They hadn't been taught the answer to this question yet.

Gavven raised his hand. "I guess we could put people who are the same in one place and people who are different in another place," he said. He didn't add that he thought that would be a very boring way to live.

The whiteshirt nodded. "That's correct, Gavven, but you shouldn't answer a question when you haven't been told what to say."

Gavven sighed. It looked as if whatever he did was going to be wrong.

Indiri smiled sympathetically. "Ms. Chang would have been glad you tried to answer on your own, Gavven," she whispered.

"I know," Gavven whispered back sadly, "but Ms. Chang isn't here."

Gavven went home on the hyperbus. Even that was different from the way it used to be. Last semester his dad or his mom had driven him to and from school in the family car. Now nobody had cars. The only way they could get from one place to another was to catch a hyperbus or walk. Everything was changing.

Gavven got off the hyperbus at the corner of Hi Street. He started to walk to his house, but suddenly stopped and stared instead. Mr. Gipps, who lived in the house on the corner, was painting his house a pale shade of purple – kind of a lavender color.

Gavven shuddered. Lavender was all right for some things. His mom had a tree that bloomed lavender-colored flowers in the spring. That looked fine. He sometimes made rainbow cakes and put pale purple icing on top. That looked delicious. His little sister, Sudeshi, wore a lavender jumpsuit sometimes. It looked all right on her. Sure, lavender was all right on flowers and cakes and on his baby sister's little jumpsuits, but not on a house.

Yuck! thought Gavven. But maybe it was the undercoat... Mr. Gipps couldn't possibly want to paint his house that weird color.

He walked on, and stopped and stared again. Mrs. Ortega from across the street was painting her house lavender, too. So were Mr. and Mrs. Jackson and the Nguyen family, who lived in houses farther down the street.

What on earth was going on? Had a hailstorm hit the area so hard that everyone in the neighborhood had to repaint their houses? But Mr. Lofgren's house was brick. It wouldn't have needed painting – even if there had been a natural disaster – yet there was Mr. Lofgren, painting away. The house was half lavender already!

The smell of paint was heavy in the air and it made Gavven want to hold his breath. Instead, he ran down the street toward his own house.

Had everyone gone nuts today?

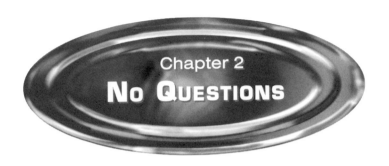

Chapter 2
NO QUESTIONS

There were cans of paint stacked up next to his own house, too. For as long as Gavven could remember, his house had been painted white. Dad used to joke about that.

"I don't like the taste of white bread," he'd say, "and I'm not very fond of snow. I want my hair to stay brown, but white is the only color for an old-fashioned clapboard house. Anything else looks ostentatious."

"What does that mean?" Gavven always asked that question, even though he knew the answer perfectly well.

"Well, a green house is envious," Dad would say with a smile. "A yellow house has a stomachache. A red house is blushing, and a blue house is gloomy. You take my word for it, Gavven, white is the only reasonable color for a house."

If Dad had said that once, he'd said it a hundred times, but now it looked as if someone else had decided lavender was the only reasonable color for a house.

Gavven ran up to his house. His mom stood staring helplessly at the cans of paint. "What's going on, Mom?"

"I have no idea," Mom replied. "A hyperbus full of whiteshirts came down the street a few hours ago and left brushes and rollers and cans of paint for everyone. I told them the house doesn't need paint, but you know what they're like!"

Gavven knew exactly what the whiteshirts were like. They were gentle and patient and they went over and over things until you did as they said. "Did they say why we have to paint the house?" he asked.

"Not exactly," Mom said. "They just said it was part of the new policy."

"What's Dad going to say?" Gavven asked. "He's not going to want to paint our house lavender."

"I don't want to paint our house lavender either," Mom said irritably. "And I'm sure you don't want to live in a lavender house, do you, Gavven?"

"Sudeshi might like it," Gavven suggested.

"Sudeshi," Mom said dryly, "is two years old. That's too young to get a vote on whether or not our house ought to be lavender."

Gavven laughed.

"Anyway," Mom said, "we better go get Sudeshi from the playplace."

"What about the paint?"

Mom shrugged. "Let's leave it here. With any luck, someone might steal it."

Gavven and Mom walked back down the street and around to the playplace on the next street. The playplace wasn't a school, but most small children went there for two or three hours each day. They enjoyed playing together with the toys and pets.

This playplace was a big brick building, but today it, too, was being painted lavender.

Mom went to talk to the playleader while Gavven looked around for his little sister. Sudeshi was hiding in the brightly colored tunnel maze, so he crawled in after her.

"I remember doing this when I was little," he told her.

She clapped her hands together. "Gavvie! Gavvie! Play little quiet mouse with me."

"It's time to go home," Gavven said. It was a tight fit in the tunnel, but he managed to turn himself around and crawl back out the way he had come. Sudeshi followed, and Gavven then carried her over to Mom.

"It's the same story here," Mom said. "The whiteshirts brought the paint and said the playplace was to be lavender from now on."

When they got back to their house, Dad had come home from work. Most of the time, Dad played on the swing set with Sudeshi as soon as he came home, but today he was glaring at the cans of paint.

"Has everyone gone crazy?" he demanded.

Mom sighed. "Apparently, it's a new law," she told him. "The whiteshirts explained that having houses that are all the same color would make things better for everyone."

"I'm sure they did," Dad snapped. "They always explain, over and over again. But saying something over and over doesn't make it right or true." He folded his arms. "I'm not going to paint our house this ridiculous color. Our house is fine the way it is."

Gavven stared. Dad didn't usually make a big deal over the new laws.

"I accepted it when they took away our cars," Dad said. "After all, cars were wasteful and inefficient. I accepted it when they took over the Glory Gate technology. I can see it should be used for the good of everyone and not for the profit of a few. I even accepted their no-meat weeks, since it meant a fairer distribution of food to other countries. But I cannot and will not accept that I have to paint my own house lavender!"

Mom, Sudeshi, and Gavven had been staring at Dad, so they all jumped when someone started clapping behind them.

"Bravo, bravo!" It was Dad's Saturday golfing friend, Mr. Lofgren, who lived next door. "I wish I were as brave as you, Dave," he said admiringly.

"I'm not being brave," Dad said. "I just can't see the point of painting our house a color I detest."

Mr. Lofgren sighed. "Lavender is supposed to be a color that makes people feel calm and tranquil," he said.

"Is that so!" Dad still sounded angry.

"Yes, indeed," Mr. Lofgren continued. "Years ago, some scientists did a whole lot of research on this subject. Apparently, they discovered that different colors can have different effects on people's moods. Red makes them aggressive, blue cools them down, yellow makes them cheerful, and this kind of a pale purple almost acts like a tranquilizer. I guess this is just part of our whiteshirted friends' new policy to make the world a more peaceful place."

Dad snorted. "I assure you it doesn't make me calm, tranquil, or peaceful. The whiteshirts are not my friends, and I am not painting my house lavender!"

"Won't you get into trouble if you don't do it?" Gavven asked.

"Probably," Dad said, "but there's nothing they can do to me... except explain it all over again, of course."

"I wish you luck, Dave," Mr. Lofgren said, "but I don't have your courage. I'm going to finish my painting."

Dad went into the house, and Mom and Gavven followed with Sudeshi.

"Don't worry, Ruth," Dad said. "All they'll do is talk to us. Remember, they are supposed to be here to make life easier, not harder."

He was almost right – the whiteshirts certainly talked. They began early the next morning, knocking at the door to ask Dad and Mom why they hadn't painted their house.

"I do not like lavender houses," Dad explained.

"All houses must be painted the regulation color," a whiteshirt said.

"I," Dad said loudly, "do not want my house to be painted a regulation color."

"All houses must be painted the regulation color," the whiteshirt repeated.

"Why?" Dad demanded. "What possible reason can you have for interfering with the color of our house?"

"No questions," the second whiteshirt said. "The house must be painted today."

"No," Dad said.

Eventually, the whiteshirts went away.

"You see, Ruth?" Dad said. "It took just one person to make a stand." Satisfied, he went off to work, leaving Gavven to catch the hyperbus to school and Mom to begin her work at home.

After the nerve-wracking business of the house painting and the whiteshirts' visit, Gavven couldn't concentrate at school. He kept answering the questions incorrectly, while Jamal gave him pitying looks.

"I can't understand why they're doing all this," Gavven said at lunchtime. "Why do they want our houses to be lavender?"

"They're just trying to make things the same for everybody, that's all," Jamal said. "It isn't fair that some people have so much more than others."

"How can trying to force me to live in a weird-looking house help other people?"

"We haven't been told the answer to that question yet," Jamal said.

"Maybe the people who make that paint are poor because they can't get anyone to buy it," Gavven suggested. "Maybe this is a plot to make people buy their paint."

"Gavven," said a whiteshirt teacher who had walked up behind them, "come to my office. Now."

Gavven shivered as he followed the whiteshirt. "I didn't do anything wrong," he said nervously.

The whiteshirt sighed. "Gavven, I have told you several times that you must not answer questions when you haven't been taught what to say."

"But I was answering my own question!" Gavven exclaimed. "Don't tell me I can't answer my own questions."

"Don't ask questions," the whiteshirt said. "Don't speculate. Do you understand that?"

Gavven didn't really understand, but he nodded anyway.

"We are making the world into a better place," the whiteshirt said. "People will realize that soon." He smiled at Gavven. "When was the last time you saw a news report that mentioned war or unrest?"

"I haven't been taught the answer to that question," Gavven said sullenly.

"There have been no such news reports since the beginning of this government's term," the whiteshirt said proudly. "You need to remember that, Gavven. Remind your father of that, as well."

Gavven went to finish his lunch, but he had lost his appetite. He tossed his sandwich in the trash.

Two shocks waited for Gavven when he got home that afternoon. The first was that his house had been painted lavender.

"But Dad said he would never paint it that color!" Gavven gasped.

"Your dad didn't do it," said Mr. Lofgren, who was standing outside with his hands in his pockets. "A squad of whiteshirts came this morning and had it all done within a couple of hours. Then they gave your mom the bill for the work."

"Dad won't like that," Gavven said.

"I don't think he will either," Mr. Lofgren said, "but I'm afraid Dave now has more to worry about than a lavender house."

"Why? What's going on?"

Mr. Lofgren looked like he was about to answer, but then he shook his head. "You better go in and find out for yourself. Oh, and tell Dave I can't play golf with him again."

"But you've always played golf with Dad!" Gavven said.

Mr. Lofgren shrugged. "Not anymore. I'm sorry, Gavven. I really am."

Gavven felt cold inside as he ran into the house. He could hear Sudeshi crying, so Mom must have picked her up from the playplace early. Or maybe she didn't go there today.

"Mom?" he called as he entered. "Hey, Mom, what's going on?"

Then Dad answered. Dad – who shouldn't have been home from work for another hour. Dad – whose face was gray.

"I lost my job," he said.

Chapter 3
SUDESHI

Gavven couldn't believe it. Dad had been working for Glory Gate Center for as long as he could remember. He had often heard Mom say that if it hadn't been for Dad and his work partner, Mr. Chang, the center might never have existed.

"The scientists may be brilliant, but we need practical people like your dad to run things," Mom was always saying. "Practical people are the ones who decide what can be done and how much it's going to cost. They're the ones who keep things moving."

But now, apparently, Glory Gate Center was going to manage without at least one of its practical people.

"Laid off!" Dad whispered bleakly. It seemed he couldn't believe it either. "The new government managers say they're streamlining the operation..."

"If you ask me, it has something to do with that stupid lavender paint," Mom said darkly. "Do you think that if you hadn't refused to paint the house, you'd still have your job?"

"I don't understand!" Dad mourned. "Has the whole world gone berserk?"

"My teacher says that the world is better now because there aren't any more wars," Gavven said.

"Did he?" Dad asked. "Were those his exact words?"

Gavven thought about it. The whiteshirts were always determined that you should remember their exact words. "Not quite," he admitted. "He said that there have been no such news reports since the beginning of this government's term, and he told me to remind you about it."

"I don't like the sound of that," Dad said.

"Neither do I," Mom said as she lifted Sudeshi to her lap. "I wish we'd painted the house ourselves. Then maybe we wouldn't be in trouble now."

Gavven decided to talk it all over with Jamal at school. Jamal might be acting a little stuck up these days, but maybe he understood a little more about what was happening. Jamal's mom and dad were nice people, but Gavven couldn't imagine them wanting to paint their house lavender, either. And if they hadn't done it, had Mr. Singh lost his job, too?

He meant to ask Jamal about that, but he didn't get the chance. When he climbed off the hyperbus the next morning, the schoolyard seemed strangely empty. There were normally about four hundred children at William Wallace Elementary School, but Gavven could see only a few of them this morning. Where was Jamal? Where was Indiri? And what about Adwoa and Tan and Mimi?

Other kids were milling around, looking for their friends.

"Where on earth is everyone?" Lukas Campbell asked.

"I can't find Adwoa! Why isn't she here yet?" complained Ellie Hauser.

Gavven shook his head. "They can't all be late for school."

The three of them walked around the school, but they couldn't find their friends.

"I really wanted to ask Jamal something," Gavven said. "He always seems to understand what the whiteshirts want."

"Wait!" Lukas stopped in his tracks and looked around again. "I think I know what's going on," he said slowly. "Have you noticed who's missing?"

"Yes, of course," Ellie said. "Adwoa."

"And Jamal and Indiri," Gavven said.

"And Tan and Mimi and Abdullah and Ali," Lukas said. He pushed back his fair hair. "There are only white people left!" he said.

"Oh!" Ellie's mouth opened in surprise. "So, where do you think our friends are? Do you think they're all out sick or something?"

"They couldn't all be sick on the same day," Gavven said. He was feeling kind of sick himself. "Do you think the whiteshirts did something to them?" he ventured. "Just because they're different?"

"Of course not!" Lukas scoffed. "The whiteshirts like Jamal. He always answers all of those stupid questions correctly."

"I bet they'll tell us what's going on," Gavven said. "As long as we don't ask questions, that is."

The others agreed, and they were right. A whiteshirt did explain.

"You've probably noticed that some of the people who used to attend this school are not here today," he said. "We've made some changes in the school system. Now, instead of 'William Wallace Elementary,' this school will be called PSW 23. That stands for 'Public School White 23.' The students who are not here today have simply transferred to other PS schools where they can be with people like themselves."

The remaining children started exchanging uneasy glances.

"Now, it isn't any of your business where any of the other children have gone, but don't worry – they are just fine," the whiteshirt said, smiling. "Later today, you will be meeting other children more like yourselves. They are going to be coming in from other parts of the city to attend PSW 23." He stood up. "All right, Gavven, let's see how well you remember the answer to that question. Where are the children who used to attend this school?"

"They've gone to other schools," Gavven said dully.

"And why are they going to other schools? Do you know, Lukas?"

"They're going to other schools so they can be with people like themselves," Lukas said.

"That's wonderful!" the whiteshirt said warmly. "You children are learning very well indeed. So, if any of your parents or other people ask about the children who used to go to this school, you will know how to answer them. There is just one more question. You have been taught the answer, but it was a few days ago. Let me see who remembers it now. Why do wars begin?"

Ellie raised her hand. "Wars begin because people are different," she answered in a singsong voice.

The whiteshirt beamed. "That's great, Ellie. Because you got the answer right, we are all going to have a treat."

The children exchanged glances. The whiteshirts didn't usually give people treats.

"We're going to watch a special video," the whiteshirt said. "It's the first video to be taken of one of the new worlds beyond Glory Gate!"

At first, they thought the video was going to be like an adventure movie, but it wasn't very good. It was shown on an old-fashioned television, and there were no stereo headsets or special speakers.

Two men and a woman walked across a grassy plain and reached a grove of tall trees.

One of the men used an axe to cut a small sapling, and a close-up shot showed the grain of the wood. The woman climbed down a bank and dipped her hand in a fast-running stream. Another close-up shot showed the water splashing against her hand and dividing around her fingers. The other man tossed things into the air and filmed them as they fell. Then he talked about air pressure and temperature. That was it – nothing exciting.

Most of the children were yawning when the video ended, but the whiteshirt was staring at the screen as if it were the most wonderful thing he had ever seen.

"Just think!" he said brightly. "There are thousands of worlds beyond Glory Gate and, so far, most of them seem to be completely uninhabited. Make sure you tell your families all about this, and inform them that this video is available for public viewing at a special screening tomorrow night."

Gavven wondered what Jamal would have thought of the film. He couldn't ask him now!

But just before it was time to go home, Gavven realized he could probably still see Jamal even if they no longer went to the same school. What about Pippin Park? Gavven sometimes met Jamal and Indiri there because it was quite close to their house.

Pippin Park was on Freedom Street, and it was full of wonderful things such as rose gardens and groves of bamboo and thick bushes. Just inside the gate, there was a thicket of bamboo that seemed to grow right against the wall. One day, Indiri and Gavven had discovered there was a small gap in the bamboo that was almost like a cave. The three friends had turned it into a hideout. It was damp, prickly, and not very comfortable, but it was a lot of fun to walk into Pippin Park and then pretend to vanish. They even had a secret code for deciding when to meet.

I bet Jamal will still go to the hideout, Gavven thought as he got on the hyperbus to go home. I'll go there this weekend and ask how he likes his new school.

He was still thinking about that and looking forward to it when he reached his street, so he felt a sense of shock all over again when he saw his newly painted house. It had been lavender the day before, of course, but somehow he had forgotten just how weird it really looked. It probably looked odd because it was so big, he thought as he went into the kitchen. A lavender-colored toy house wouldn't have looked nearly as bad.

Mom was in the kitchen, watching as Dad chopped up carrots and potatoes. It was a no-meat week, so they were having vegetables for dinner. Sudeshi was playing on the floor with some cardboard tubes and a little model horse that had once belonged to Gavven.

"Didn't Sudi go to the playplace today?" Gavven asked.

Mom glanced up. "Oh, hi, Gavv. No, I didn't take her there today."

"Why not?" Gavven bent down and hoisted Sudeshi into the air. "Sudeshi loves going to the playplace, don't you, Sudi?"

Sudeshi laughed and tugged at Gavven's ears. "Gavvie play, Gavvie play," she chanted.

Gavven peered at his sister's laughing face. "She isn't sick or anything, is she?"

"No. I got a call this morning saying the playplace was closed today while they finish the painting. I suppose they don't want the little ones getting covered in lavender paint."

"I'd have thought the whiteshirts would love that," Gavven said. "It would make the children all look the same."

Mom glanced at him sharply. "They're not talking about that again, are they?"

"Mom, that's all they ever seem to talk about." Gavven put Sudeshi down and picked up a piece of carrot.

Dad tossed the rest of the carrots into the dinnermaker, which began to grind noisily.

It seemed strange to have Dad home so early in the day, but Gavven didn't mention it. Neither did Mom or Dad.

Dinner was a quiet meal, except when Gavven told Mom and Dad that Jamal and Indiri and many of his other friends were now going to a different school.

Dad said nothing, but he angrily shoved his carrots around on the plate in front of him.

"The whole world seems to be changing," Mom said sadly. She took Sudeshi's spoon and began to help her with her chopped vegetables. "Just a few years ago, they were encouraging everyone to mix with each other so there were different kinds of people all living and working together."

There was a knock on the door. "Would you go see who that is, Gavv?" Mom said.

There were two whiteshirts, a man and a woman, outside the door. The woman consulted a tiny computer she was carrying, then smiled at Gavven. "Gavven Janus?"

"Yes."

"Do you live here with your parents, Davit and Rutha Janus?"

"That's right."

"Does a female child, known as Sudeshi Janus, live here with you?"

"She's my sister." Gavven was puzzled. He glanced over his shoulder. Dad was still spearing carrots and Mom was scraping out the last of Sudeshi's bowl of vegetables.

The female whiteshirt smiled again. "Do you mind if we come in? We won't keep you more than a few minutes."

Gavven stood back automatically and the whiteshirts walked past him into the kitchen. Mom was frowning and Dad grew pale.

"What do you want?" Dad didn't sound very friendly.

"Davit and Rutha Janus?"

"That's right," Mom said.

The whiteshirts were still smiling. "We have a requisition order," the man said.

"What for? You're not taking our house, are you?" Mom asked.

The whiteshirts shook their heads. "That is not why we are here today, Mrs. Janus."

"Then what do you want?"

"We've come for the child," the female whiteshirt said.

Mom, Dad, and Gavven all gasped.

"Give us the little girl."

Chapter 4
NILSTATE

Sudeshi was sitting in her high chair, smiling at the strangers. The woman walked over to remove her from the chair, but Mom stepped between them.

The man, acting as if he didn't notice that there was a problem, showed Dad the mini-com screen. "You'll find the requisition is all in order," he said. "You just need to pack Sudeshi's clothing – you will be reimbursed for its cost, of course."

"The government is even prepared to pay you for the food she's eaten over the past eighteen months," the woman said proudly.

"You can't take her," Mom said in a dazed voice. "She's our daughter."

"Yes we can," the woman said. "You see, because this little girl has Indian heritage, she is not your blood relation and therefore she cannot be a member of your family."

"This is the most ridiculous thing I have ever heard!" Mom said. "You cannot take her from us – she's ours!" With that, she lifted Sudeshi from the high chair and clutched her tightly to her chest.

"Sudeshi is our legal daughter," Dad said. "Her adoption papers were signed eighteen months ago."

"This order supersedes all such adoptions," the woman said. "Sudeshi will be much better off when we relocate her with a suitable family."

"What do you mean 'suitable'?" Mom gasped, fighting back tears. "What do you mean 'better off'? What is better for a child than to stay with a family who loves her and wants to keep her more than anything?"

"Sudeshi will be settled with an Indian family," the male whiteshirt said. "Now, go pack her clothing, Mrs. Janus."

"She's already settled with *our* family," Dad said, as he moved between the whiteshirts and Mom and Sudeshi. "She is *our* daughter. You can't take her away."

"Actually, we *can* take her," the female whiteshirt said. "Under this new policy, she will be brought up in the correct environment with people of her own kind."

Mom and Dad argued fiercely, but the whiteshirts were determined.

"This is the law, Mr. and Mrs. Janus," the man said mechanically. "If you don't hand her over, we will take her by force. Don't make us do that. It would upset the child."

By now, both Sudeshi and Mom were crying, and Dad was fighting back tears. Gavven was so upset, he didn't know where to look, but he also had an idea. He tugged at Mom's sleeve.

"Mom?" His voice sounded husky, but he managed to attract her attention. "Mom, ask them if Sudi can go stay with the Singhs. You know, Jamal's mom and dad?"

"Sudeshi isn't going anywhere," Mom sobbed, clutching Sudeshi even tighter. "You people are monsters – I would never hand a child over to you!"

"Well, that's just about enough of that, Mrs. Janus. You are not doing yourself or the child any favors by acting this way," the male whiteshirt said over the sound of the little girl's screams. He turned to Gavven. "Do you have something to suggest, Gavven?"

"Yes!" Gavven said. "If you're going to take her away, will you take her to Mr. and Mrs. Singh? They live near Pippin Park and Sudi knows them. Jamal's grandparents came from India, so the family looks like Sudi."

A flicker of thought crossed the whiteshirt's face. "I'm sure that can be arranged," he said, "if the Singh family agrees."

"They'll agree," Gavven told him urgently. "Jamal is my best friend. We used to go to the same school."

"Because our government has your best interests at heart, there should be no problems with putting the child with the Singh family. We will process this request," the man said. "If all parties do not agree, we will make other arrangements."

"Please – I beg you – leave her here until you find out," Mom said desperately, but the whiteshirts refused.

"We can't do that, Mrs. Janus. You might hide the child somewhere," the man said.

"I don't know why you didn't just steal her away from the playplace!" Dad muttered as he stroked Sudeshi's glossy black hair.

"That wouldn't have been fair," the female whiteshirt said.

"Fair? Fair?" Mom cried. "What do you care about being fair?"

"Let go of the child, Mrs. Janus," the male whiteshirt said, wrestling Sudeshi out of Mom's clutching arms. "Pack her clothes as quickly as possible and send them to the nearest playplace. We'll pick them up there."

Carrying Sudeshi, the whiteshirts left. The kitchen still rang with the child's cries.

Mom sank to the floor, her hands covering her eyes. "How could you let them take her!" she sobbed at Dad.

"Ruth, you know these people as well as I do – there is no way to stop them," he said hopelessly.

Gavven realized he was shaking. This was the worst day of his entire life. Since the big government changeover, many other days had been strange or uncomfortable or annoying. But this was horrible!

"Mom?" He went over and hugged her. "We'll still be able to see her."

"No, we won't," Mom gasped as she wept. "Those vicious whiteshirts will see to that. I haven't seen the Singhs for days. I used to run into Jamilla Singh when I was out running errands, but not anymore."

"Jamal, Indiri, and I have a hideout in Pippin Park," Gavven said. "I'm sure they'll bring her there to see us."

Mom wiped her sleeve across her eyes. "I'm going to call the Singhs right now."

"Ruth, don't," Dad said quietly. "The whiteshirts will be expecting that." He glanced around and motioned for Mom and Gavven to come closer. "Listen! This is the last straw and if I'd known it would come to this, I would have spoken to you sooner."

"Spoken to us about what?" Gavven asked.

"What I've been planning." Dad sighed. "I'd like to think we could fight this thing and win, but you know that isn't possible. I tried to fight the whiteshirts over painting the house and look what happened!"

"They just painted the house themselves," Gavven said.

"Yes, and I lost my job. Fighting them doesn't work, but there is one thing we can do. We can leave."

"We're not going to go anywhere without Sudeshi," Mom said, the hysteria rising again in her voice.

"I wouldn't dream of going anywhere without Sudeshi." Dad looked straight at Gavven. "Look, Gavv, I'm going to tell you something, and you need to keep absolutely quiet about it. Do you understand? We're going to get Sudeshi back and go away from here. We'll go somewhere they'll never find us, but until we do that, we have to carry on as usual."

"How can we?" Mom asked.

"Look, I know this isn't going to be easy," Dad said. "The whiteshirts already think we're troublemakers, so we just need to keep on making enough trouble that they think everything is normal, but not so much that it causes them to come down on us any harder. I'll send the World Government Office a petition to get Sudi back. We'll look like we're getting ready to fight this as hard as possible."

"What will we really be doing?" Gavven asked. For some reason, he was starting to feel the first stirrings of hope he had experienced in months.

"We'll be watching for our chance," Dad said. "We'll get Sudi back and then we'll all escape through Glory Gate."

"Escape through Glory Gate? How? When?"

"As soon as we have the chance," Dad said. He sat down. "Listen, Ruth. I've never said very much about Glory Gate, have I?"

Mom shook her head.

"You always said you'd promised not to say anything about it," Gavven said.

"So I did. Well, normally I wouldn't break a promise, but I think the whiteshirts and the people they work for are doing something far worse than breaking promises."

"They say they're trying to make things better," Gavven said doubtfully.

"I'm sure that's exactly what they are saying – maybe there are even a few of them who believe it. The thing is, they have become addicted to their power and have forgotten what they were elected to do. They're messing around with things that were fine just the way they were. They've become tyrants and bullies, and their main goal seems to be to prevent us from thinking for ourselves."

Gavven thought about Jamal. He'd stopped thinking for himself. Instead, he believed what the whiteshirts told him without ever wondering if it made any sense.

"So," Dad continued, "I'm going to tell you about Glory Gate. You have a right to know. For one thing, it isn't exactly a gate."

"Then what is it?" Gavven asked.

"It's a machine that smashes particles of atoms," Dad said. "There have been machines like that for a while, but Glory Gate is much more efficient. It smashes the particles so completely that it creates something called 'Nilstate.' That's just another name for 'nothing place.' It isn't really nothing; it's just a place where everything is very thin."

"Like out in space?" Gavven asked. It felt strange to be asking questions again.

"Not exactly, Gavv." Dad frowned as he tried to explain. "You know how rock is more dense than soil?"

Gavven nodded. "You can dig holes in soil, but not in rock."

"Good!" Dad said. "Now, soil is more dense than water. Right?"

"You can move through water, but you can't just move through soil," Gavven said.

"That's right. And water," Dad continued, "is more dense than air."

"Yes!" Gavven felt almost happy again as he began to understand. "You can float in water, but not in air."

"Exactly!" Dad said. "Well, air is more dense than Nilstate."

"You've lost me again," Gavven said.

"You can travel through space – which is basically like traveling through air – to other planets," Dad said. "With Nilstate, you don't travel through anything. You break down into Nilstate at the gate and are simply put back together as your normal self in another world."

Gavven felt as if his mind were stretching as he tried to understand. "How do you know where you are going to end up? How come you don't just end up floating in space somewhere?"

"Glory Gate can be programmed almost like a rocket," Dad said. "You just figure out the coordinates of a place you want to go and Glory Gate is programmed to take you out of Nilstate when you reach that specific location."

"So how does this help us?" Mom asked. "Even if we could get to a Glory Gate, those whiteshirts would just come after us and bring us back."

"Well, if we used Glory Gate like everybody else does, that would definitely happen," Dad said. "The thing is, before I was fired, I was on a team that developed a program for Glory Gate to send travelers to worlds that match the conditions we need to live. If I just set the Gate to random, no one will know exactly where we went."

"When can we go?" Gavven couldn't wait for this new adventure.

"We will leave just as soon as we get Sudeshi back," Dad said. "And as soon as I have the chance to find a Glory Gate generator." He turned to Gavven. "Gavv? You know you cannot discuss this with anyone else? If you do, it might get back to the whiteshirts. If that happens, our chance will never come."

"I understand," Gavven said.

Chapter 5
MIDNIGHT VISITOR

After that, Gavven and his family did their best to live their lives as normally as possible. It was very difficult, especially considering how much they missed Sudeshi.

Dad and Mom wrote letters and sent e-mail to the government, insisting that they get Sudeshi back. In other words, they made a nuisance of themselves, but not too much of a nuisance.

Gavven tried to seem invisible at school. Every time a whiteshirt spoke to him, he jumped. He was certain they knew what he was thinking. It almost would have been easier if the whiteshirts had been cruel to him, but they never got irritated. Instead, they just kept repeating their motto: "Things will soon be better for everyone."

Then, one day as he came home from school, Gavven saw the male whiteshirt who had taken Sudeshi waiting for him on the front steps of his house.

"Hello, Gavven!" the whiteshirt said heartily. "It looks like you are the first one home today. Do you know if your mother has packed the little Indian girl's clothes yet?"

Gavven shook his head. He was almost afraid to speak.

"Please ask her to do it when she gets home," the whiteshirt said. He smiled at Gavven. "By the way, you'll be happy to know the little girl is very happy with the Singh family. I visited her today."

"Okay," Gavven said. He didn't know what else to say. He supposed it might even be true. Sudeshi might be happy with the Singhs. She knew them, and Indiri was always kind to her.

But she was definitely happy with us, Gavven thought rebelliously. She's my sister, not Indiri's sister or Jamal's sister. Anyway, if the Singhs had wanted a little girl, they would have had one themselves. Or they would have adopted a child the way we did.

He wondered if he should tell Mom what the whiteshirt had said.

That night, Gavven woke up to hear someone talking quietly out in the kitchen. He thought it was Mom and Dad. They hadn't slept well since they'd lost Sudeshi. He tried to go back to sleep, but after a while, he realized there was someone else in the house.

Was it a whiteshirt? Mr. Lofgren? The Singhs? Had they brought Sudeshi for a visit?

Gavven couldn't hear more than the murmur of voices, so he quietly got out of bed and crept out to the kitchen door.

Now he could hear a little more, but it still didn't make sense. He peeked in the door.

Mom and Dad were sitting at the table drinking coffee, and Gavven realized he knew the third person. It was Mr. Chang, who had worked with Dad at the Glory Gate Center.

The door creaked and Mr. Chang put down his coffee cup with a clunk. "Who's there?" He sounded nervous.

"It's just Gavven," Dad said reassuringly.

Gavven came into the kitchen and Mr. Chang smiled at him.

"Hello, Gavven. I just dropped by to have a cup of coffee with your parents. Wow, look how late it is! I really should get going."

Gavven glanced at the clock. It was midnight. Mr. Chang was looking guilty, as if he'd been caught doing something wrong.

"Don't panic, Samm," Dad said. "Gavven knows some of what's going on, so he might as well hear the rest." Dad reached out and pulled up another chair. "Sit down, Gavv. Mr. Chang has some news for us."

"Good news or bad news?" Gavven asked.

"That depends," Mr. Chang said. He normally had a cheerful face, but at the moment he wasn't smiling.

"Go on," Mom said. She was holding her coffee cup tightly.

Mr. Chang nodded. "As you know, I still work at the Glory Gate Center," he said. "And there's talk at the center – disturbing talk."

"I'm not surprised," Dad said grimly. "What is it now?"

Mr. Chang cleared his throat. "It seems that the whiteshirts are very pleased with the results of their segregation policy," he said.

"What's segregation?" Gavven asked.

"It means putting things into separate piles," Dad said. "Or in this case, it's the way the whiteshirts have separated all the different kinds of people into different groups. All the Indian children are in one school, all the Chinese people are schooled somewhere else. Segregation is part of their big effort to keep those groups of people from getting together."

"That's right," Mr. Chang said. "As of this week, only people who look like me are allowed to work at the center. Everyone else had to go to other jobs somewhere else."

"Except for me," Dad said with a grim chuckle. "I'm sure that's because I gave them trouble over the stupid paint."

"Well, you're not missing anything good," Mr. Chang said. "The whiteshirts are so determined to complete their plan that they've decided to take the final step soon – before any unrest or opposition has a chance to build."

"What's the final step?" Gavven asked.

Mr. Chang looked around nervously. "First, they are going to create different sections around the city that will match sections they are creating all over the rest of the planet. When that happens, I won't be able to visit you and you won't be able to visit me – or anyone except people of your own racial group. The final step will be a plan to keep different kinds of people away from one another permanently."

"How will they do that?" Mom asked, frowning. "Even if they sent them to other countries, they could always come back on planes or ships."

"They're going to send racially based groups of people through Glory Gate," Mr. Chang said quietly. "Each different race of human will be sent to a different planet in a different dimension."

Mom gasped. "They can't do that! They can't send people away from their homes!"

"They took Sudeshi away," Gavven reminded her. "And Dad was going to..." He stopped talking suddenly as he remembered he'd promised not to mention Dad's plans to anyone at all.

"I'm afraid they *can* do it and they *will* do it," Mr. Chang said. "In some ways, it isn't such a bad idea. It would certainly solve our problem of overpopulation here on Earth. Who knows? Maybe they're right when they say it would prevent any more wars."

"Nonsense!" Mom snorted. "If you only have one race of people, they will still find something to fight about. Right-handed people would fight left-handed people, or people who work with their hands would decide they hate people who write computer programs. Or meat eaters would fight vegetarians."

"Perhaps," Mr. Chang said. "However, the whiteshirts seem to think it's worth the risk. After they've sent the different races through Nilstate, they're going to destroy the Glory Gate technology so no one can come back."

"Wouldn't the scientists just build it again?" Gavven asked.

"Not if they're split up and deprived of vast power resources," Mr. Chang said.

"What about the people who are forced to live in other dimensions for the rest of their lives?" Mom persisted. "It isn't fair to them, is it? There won't be any roads or houses or even crops of food for them."

"They'll have the resources to create them," Mr. Chang said. "The people who stay in this dimension won't have the chance for a fresh start, although they'll have the advantage of living in existing cities. Civilizations will begin all over again, and each will develop in its own way."

"That's all very well for people like us," Dad said, "but Ruth's right. It will be difficult for the people who are sent through Nilstate. I would hate having to start all over again in another world." Dad looked warningly at Gavven, to let him know not to blurt out their secret.

So, Gavven thought, Dad hasn't told Mr. Chang anything about our plans. Is he afraid Mr. Chang might give them away?

Mr. Chang was looking puzzled. "What do you mean by that, Dave? You will be one of those who will be sent away."

"Oh, come on!" Dad said. "We'll be the ones who stay!"

"Why would you think that?"

"Well..." Dad looked sheepish. "I guess I just figured we would."

"The whiteshirts are the same race as we are," Gavven pointed out. "They made Indian people like the Singhs and black people like Adwoa go to other schools, but they didn't send people like us to different places."

"So you think the whiteshirts want to keep this old world to themselves and people who look like them!" Mr. Chang said.

"Well, sure," Dad said. "It seems obvious."

Mr. Chang laughed. "No, people of my race will be the ones who stay on this old world. The whiteshirts are moving their people, including your family, through Nilstate."

"But why?"

"There are more of us than there are of you," Mr. Chang said simply. "Therefore, your race will be easier to move. It's all very practical."

"But what about Sudeshi?" Mom said.

"People like Sudeshi will be sent through Nilstate as well, but it won't be to the same planet or dimension as yours." Mr. Chang sighed, and patted Mom's shoulder. "I'm very sorry, Ruth. I wish I could have brought you better news."

Dad, Mom, and Mr. Chang stayed around the table talking for a long time, but Gavven went back to bed. He had to be in school in the morning, and if he didn't show up, the whiteshirts would come to see why he hadn't.

A few days later, the whiteshirts called a public meeting in Civility Square. They invited only white people, so there was no chance for Gavven's family to see the Singhs or Mr. Chang.

"We bring you the most wonderful news!" announced the whiteshirt in charge of the meeting. "Thanks to Glory Gate technology, we are all going to receive new homes! Your government is working out the final details, so pack your belongings and we will send you final instructions through your vidvision sets."

An amazed murmur swept through the crowd, but no one asked any questions. They had all learned that questions wouldn't be answered. The whiteshirts would tell people only what they wanted them to know.

"Of course," the whiteshirt continued, "there is no question of bringing people from Africa and China to the Glory Gate Center we have here. Because our government wants life to be fair for everyone, it is mass-producing Glory Gate generators around the world. Then, all white people will join together and go to the same new home.

"This is a wonderful day in the history of humankind! We will all be together in a new home, in our new world. There will be no more wars!"

The whiteshirt sounded so happy that a lot of people in Civility Square began to look happy, too.

"This may be for the best," someone said.

"Life will be better for everyone," someone else agreed.

"We'll be with people like ourselves. Things will be so much easier."

Soon cheers of approval were breaking out from the crowd, encouraged by whiteshirts who were shouting and applauding. Gavven noticed that Dad was grinding his teeth, but Mom jabbed him in the ribs with her elbow until he began to cheer with the rest.

Now that Gavven knew they would be leaving so soon, he was afraid they would never see Sudeshi again.

It was all very well for Dad to say he'd get Sudeshi back, but how? When they tried to visit the Singhs, they were turned back by whiteshirt guards, who said the street where the Singhs lived was only for people like them. There was a boundary that no one was allowed to cross. When Mom tried to call Mrs. Singh on the telephone, a whiteshirt broke in on the line and told her she was not allowed to converse with people outside of her boundary area.

Worst of all, even if they got Sudeshi back, they would never be allowed to take her to their new home. Mom was crying all the time, and Gavven felt raw and skinned inside.

One day, a few weeks after the public meeting, Gavven saw some people who looked like Mr. Chang. They were clearly of Chinese descent, and they were dressed just like whiteshirts, except their shirts were yellow. They must have seen him, but they marched right past him as if he didn't exist.

"Yellowshirts," Dad said when Gavven told him about it. "That makes sense. If all the whiteshirts are going to a new dimension, they must be setting up a new government for the people who stay here."

"There will be blackshirts, too, for people of African descent," Mom said sadly. "And brownshirts and redshirts and all kinds of other colored shirts. There will be a new government for every new dimension."

Gavven shivered. "When are they going to make us go?" he asked. "And what about Sudeshi?"

"We'll get her back, Gavven," Dad said, but he looked scared. "When we do, Samm Chang has a plan."

"What is it?"

"I'd better not tell you just yet," Dad said. "But do you remember when Mr. Chang came to visit us? He told us something after you went to bed. Apparently, we're not the only people who have problems with the new government plan."

"But we'll get Sudeshi first," Mom insisted.

Gavven decided he was just going to have to do something himself. The whiteshirts were watching Dad and Mom constantly. He hoped they wouldn't pay any attention to a kid.

So he started to plan. First, he offered to do the grocery shopping for Mom and Dad. He bought bread, fruit, carrots, beans, coffee, flour, and sugar. He also bought some food coloring – just the basic red, yellow, and blue.

The next day, Gavven got up early to beat his parents to the kitchen. He poured the three small bottles of food coloring into a small jar. He capped the jar tightly and shook it up. In no time at all, they had mixed into a kind of warm brown color. Slipping the jar into his jacket, he crept out the front door.

Instead of walking over to the hyperbus he normally took to school, he ambled casually over to a small patch of trees near the Indian boundary. There, he hid in some dense bushes and painted his face and hands with the brown dye he had made. He pulled a stocking cap out of his pocket and put it on over his light-brown hair.

When he emerged, he was able to cross the boundary into the Indian section without anyone stopping him. He then walked to

Pippin Park, crawled into his old hideout, and waited.

It was a very long day, but eventually he saw the hyperbus from Jamal's new school go past. Sure enough, Jamal and Indiri got off the hyperbus and came through the gate into Pippin Park. Excellent – they were still using the shortcut home!

Gavven crept out of the hideout and walked toward them. "Jamal?"

Jamal turned to wave, then he suddenly dropped his hand and stared instead. "Who are you?"

"It's me. Gavven Janus."

Indiri gasped and smiled welcomingly, but Jamal just shook his head and turned away.

"Jamal, please. I have to talk to you."

"Our people don't talk to your people. We're different. Wars begin because people are different."

"Jamal, we want to see Sudeshi. Please?" Gavven was embarrassed to find that his voice was shaking.

"Sudeshi can't have anything to do with you. She is different from you. Wars begin because people are different," Jamal said mechanically.

"Sudeshi is my little sister and I love her!" Gavven choked.

This wasn't the way he wanted things to go, but what else could he say? Jamal was looking at him as if he were a dangerous stranger.

"Go away," Jamal commanded. "Go wash that stuff off your face. You shouldn't pretend you're like us. You're nothing like us."

"Please?" Gavven begged, but Jamal simply walked away.

"Come on, Indiri. Let's go home."

Indiri followed Jamal, but not before she glanced back at Gavven. She smiled at him and lifted her hand as if she were going to wave. Then she tapped the watch she wore on her wrist and held up five fingers.

"Come on, Indiri!" Jamal snapped, and she hurried after him.

Gavven gave a shaky sigh. Indiri didn't hate him. Indiri understood. She had even used their old code for meeting at the hideout!

Five fingers. She meant she would meet him at five a.m.

Gavven started for home. He was grateful that the whiteshirts hadn't set up fences or checkpoints at the boundaries. He knew he could avoid the patrols – he just didn't think he could fool someone who was looking at him close-up.

Halfway home, he hid in the small group of trees again and used some of his mom's face scrub, which he had removed from the bathroom cabinet that morning. He had to get the food coloring off his skin before some whiteshirt saw him and sent him back to the Indian section.

"Where have you been?" Mom snapped when he walked in the door. "The whiteshirts were here claiming you didn't go to school today.

They kept asking where you were and I couldn't tell them because I didn't know."

"I went to Pippin Park instead," Gavven told her eagerly.

"You couldn't have," Mom said, amazed. "The whiteshirts won't let you go over the boundary. Neither will the brownshirts."

"I made myself look like Jamal," Gavven said. He showed Mom the hat he had worn and the streaks of brown food coloring that were left on his hands.

"Gavven!" Mom's face suddenly blazed with hope. "Did you get to see Sudeshi?"

"No. I stayed in the park," Gavven said. "I saw Jamal and Indiri on their way home from school. Sudi doesn't go to school, so of course she wasn't with them."

"Didn't you go home with them? Didn't you ask them to bring Sudi to you?"

"I couldn't," Gavven said. "Jamal wouldn't talk to me." He looked down unhappily. "Jamal has learned all the right answers, Mom. He's not my friend anymore."

"Oh." Mom looked as if she were about to start crying.

"Indiri didn't say anything," Gavven said. "She just sort of waved, but she gave me a signal." He explained to Mom about the hideout meeting signal. "Indiri wants me to meet her early tomorrow morning at the hideout."

"Gavven!" Mom gave him a hug. "Do you think she might bring Sudeshi?"

"I hope so. I can't see any other reason why she would try to meet me there."

"We all have to go along," Mom said firmly. "Do you have enough of that brown dye to disguise Dad and me?"

Chapter 7
HIDING IN PLAIN SIGHT

Dad wanted to wait and try to firm up their escape plan first so they could leave as soon as they had Sudeshi, but there was no way they could let Indiri know that.

"If I don't turn up, she won't know what's going on," Gavven said. "If I go and try to arrange for her to come back another time, Jamal might find out and stop her."

It hurt Gavven to think of Jamal as an enemy, but he knew he had to. Jamal had learned all the right answers and he was sure to tell the brownshirts if he discovered what Indiri planned to do.

"What about Indiri? Do you really think she is on our side?" Mom asked suddenly as the three of them crept through the dark the next morning. There was no one around, but they were still careful to put on their disguises before they reached the boundary.

"Indiri won't tell," Gavven said.

"Won't she get in trouble?" Mom asked.

Dad took Mom's hand. "I don't think so, Ruth. They won't hurt her. The whiteshirts never hurt anyone."

"They never even get mad," Gavven said. "They just repeat things over and over and over again until you give up."

"The Janus family will never give up!" Dad said grandly.

Indiri was already at the hideout when they arrived. Gavven could just see the shape of her crouched among the bamboo stems.

"Indiri?" he called softly.

"Indiri?" Mom echoed.

There was a rustling noise and Indiri stood up and began to back away. She edged out of the bamboo and then, suddenly, she turned and ran.

"Indiri!" Mom cried. "It's just us – Gavven's family! Come back!"

Indiri vanished into the darkness of the early morning, but Gavven could hear something else rustling in the bamboo.

He ducked into the hideout and there, curled in a nest of blankets, was Sudeshi.

Gavven picked her up and hugged her. "Sudi, it's me, Gavv," he whispered as she began to whimper.

"Gavvie?" Sudeshi sounded doubtful, and then very cranky. "Gavvie go way!"

"No," Gavven said, smiling with relief. "Sudi went away. Now Sudi is coming home again with Gavvie."

Mom and Dad were crowding into the hideout, and for a few minutes there was a lot of hugging and kissing. Mom burst into tears and Sudeshi started to cry, too.

"We'd better go," Gavven said. "The sky's getting light."

There was already a streak of dawn in the east and soon the street would be full of people and hyperbuses.

"Now what?" Mom asked as they left Pippin Park.

"We have to get across the boundary again and clean off this brown dye before we get caught," Dad said.

"What about Sudi?" Gavven asked when they had scrubbed their faces as clean as they could. The sun was up, and he could see his little sister's jet black hair and dark skin quite plainly. "I didn't even think of bringing any white powder or a hat for her."

"It wouldn't have worked anyway," Mom said. She glanced at her watch. "Oh dear – it's almost seven o'clock! We'll just wrap her up and hope no one notices her."

Dad wrapped a blanket around Sudeshi. "Ssh!" he whispered when she protested. "Pretend to be a little quiet mouse, Sudi."

Sudeshi smiled. She liked playing the little quiet mouse game.

Dad tucked her under his arm, and they strolled toward home – moving fast but not too fast. The curtains in the lavender houses were opening, and people were coming out their front doors. Several times, the family saw whiteshirt patrols, but luckily none came near enough to ask any questions.

Suddenly, they saw the hyperbuses for the schoolchildren start driving past.

Mom gasped. "We have to get home so Gavven doesn't miss school again!"

They began to hurry, but as they approached their house, they realized they were already too late. One whiteshirt was waiting on the sidewalk and another was knocking at the door.

"They're on to us!" Mom gasped. "They know we have Sudeshi!"

"No," Dad whispered. "I think they're here to make sure Gavven gets on the hyperbus."

"Daddy!" Sudeshi squirmed.

"Little quiet mouse, Sudi!" Gavven said desperately. "Little quiet mouse!"

"Sudi walk."

"No." Dad thought fast. "Gavven, run home and say you went for a walk. Then get on the hyperbus for school. Be polite. Do whatever they want. Mom and I will take Sudi somewhere safe."

"No!" Mom said. "We all have to stick together!"

"Listen, Ruth," Dad said sharply. "We have to act naturally. Go on, Gavv. Come home as usual after school. I'll be waiting for you – and if not, there'll be a message."

Gavven swallowed hard, then he walked up to the house. The whiteshirt at the gate looked up as he approached. "Hello, Gavven," he said pleasantly. "Where have you been?"

"Out for a walk," Gavven said. "I'm just about to catch the hyperbus."

"That's right," the whiteshirt said. "You missed school yesterday." He smiled. "Come along. We'll ride there with you."

"Just a moment," the other whiteshirt said, turning away from the door. "Where's your mother, Gavven? We need to pick up the little Indian girl's clothes since she hasn't dropped them off for us yet."

"Mom isn't home," Gavven said quickly.

"I suppose she went for a walk," the whiteshirt said. "And what about your father, Gavven? Has he gone for a walk, too?"

Gavven licked his lips.

"I really need to see your parents, Gavven," the whiteshirt said in the same friendly voice. "Let's see if we can find them before we catch the hyperbus."

"We won't have to look far," the first whiteshirt said, holding a hand to his ear. "I have a radio report that Davit and Rutha Janus are just around the corner from here."

"I don't think they could be," Gavven said desperately. "I think they walked over to visit some friends on Feather Street."

"Feather Street is beyond the Chinese boundary," the whiteshirt said pleasantly. "They can't be there, Gavven. Why are you lying to us?"

Gavven shook his head. Polite and normal, he thought. Just be polite and normal.

"I have to go in to get my lunch," he said. He walked casually past the whiteshirts and into the house.

Now what? They'd come in after him in a moment... Gavven punched the noisy dinnermaker into action and left it running while he dashed out the back door and climbed over the fence. Crouching low, he raced after Mom and Dad down the street that ran behind the houses.

"Quick!" he gasped. "They're going to be coming after you!"

There wasn't time to think of a plan. Dad grabbed Mom's hand and Mom grabbed Gavven's and they began to run along the street. A hyperbus was approaching, so Dad signaled for it to stop.

"This isn't my bus!" Gavven protested breathlessly.

"We don't want your bus," Dad said. "We just want to get away from here."

They boarded and the hyperbus shot away again, hurtling past the two whiteshirts as they ran back along Gavven's street.

"They'll call ahead," Dad whispered. "We better get off at the next stop."

"That's near the Chinese boundary," Mom hissed, but Dad shrugged.

"I know, but it can't be helped. At least there are plenty of people there. There's a place we can go."

As soon as the hyperbus slid to a halt, they jumped out and began to run again, down through the tangle of streets that led to the marketplace. There were a lot of people walking there, but no hyperbuses. The streets were too narrow and crooked for them to fit.

"Where are we going?" Mom whispered as people turned to stare at them.

"To Wing Terrace." Dad's voice was low and Gavven could hardly hear him above the sound of their running feet.

"The terrace? It's been boarded up for years and years."

"Ssh." Dad glanced over his shoulder and dropped to a walk. "If we keep running, we'll attract more attention."

Breathing hard, they wandered through the twisty paths of the marketplace, trying to look as if they were out for a day's shopping.

"If anyone asks why you're not at school, Gavv, pretend you're sick," Mom said.

Carefully, they worked their way past the market to the ancient Victorian terrace, which was basically a wall made of lots of tall, narrow houses joined together. The houses looked battered and drab, and there was a ratty sign outside forbidding entry.

Gavven's heart was still pounding, even though they'd stopped running. If the whiteshirts caught them now, they'd take Sudeshi away. They'd make sure his family never had a second chance to get her back. And once they'd all been sent through Glory Gate, they'd never see Sudeshi again.

Their feet seemed to crunch loudly on the cracked, broken sidewalk as Dad glanced at the boarded-up doors of the terrace. "I don't want to knock," he whispered. "I hope someone's keeping watch..."

"What's going on?" Gavven asked. He was pretty sure they hadn't come to Wing Terrace by chance.

Just as he asked that question, the door of one of the houses swung open, and someone beckoned urgently from the shadows. "Dave, Ruth... in here!"

"Quick!" Dad practically leapt into the doorway, and Mom and Gavven followed. The door closed behind them, with the boards still nailed across the front of it.

"I've been expecting you," Mr. Chang said.

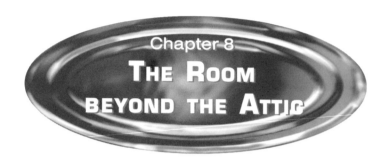

Chapter 8

THE ROOM
BEYOND THE ATTIC

Mom stared. "What are you doing here, Samm? This is Caucasian territory."

"Never mind that," Mr. Chang said. "Come with me, Ruth – quickly." He smiled over his shoulder. "Did you get your daughter back?"

Dad grinned. "Of course! We wouldn't be here if we hadn't."

"How'd you know we were coming?" Mom demanded.

Mr. Chang touched his ear. "I have a whiteshirt radio-frequency earpiece. They're pretty interested in the Janus family today."

Mr. Chang led them up two flights of very steep stairs. The carpets were tattered and the whole place reeked of dust and mildew. "Sorry about the surroundings," Mr. Chang said. "We can't have the place looking too populated."

He opened a low door leading into the attic. There was a stack of moldy cardboard boxes against the wall, and Mr. Chang ducked around the side of them. "It's kind of a tight squeeze here," he said cheerfully.

Mom grimaced, and grabbed Sudeshi from Dad's arms. "Dave, you help Gavven."

Gavven followed Dad behind the stack of boxes. From the front, it looked as if the stack was leaning right up against the wall, but there was a narrow space behind. Gavven was reminded of the hideout in Pippin Park.

Behind the boxes was another door, which Mr. Chang opened with some difficulty. "Here we are," he said, and stepped through.

Gavven blinked. It wasn't exactly bright in the room beyond the attic, but it was a lot brighter than the musty area behind him. The room was enormous! It was long and narrow, stacked with boxes and bundles and crates, and teeming with people.

Behind him, he heard Mom's amazed voice. "What's going on here?"

"We made this room by knocking all the attics together into one long hall," Mr. Chang said. "It makes a good storage space and a meeting hall, and it's ideal for people like yourselves who need to keep out of the whiteshirts' way."

A small elderly woman came out of the crowd, a smile splitting her round, wrinkled face. It was Gavven's old teacher, Ms. Chang. "Hello, my dears," she said, and held out her hand to Gavven. "Hello, Gavven! I hope you haven't forgotten how to think!"

Gavven smiled back. He was confused. "What are you doing here?" he asked.

Ms. Chang shook her head. "I'm here with my son," she said, pointing to Mr. Chang. "Samm used to work with your dad, remember? He's been planning to leave this old world and since he's my only relative, I'm going with him. Besides," she sniffed, "I think you'll need a teacher in your new world.

You'll certainly need to know how to use that brain of yours... that is, if your family decides to come with us."

"But you don't have to go!" Gavven said. "Isn't that what Mr. Chang said?"

"Of course we don't have to go," Ms. Chang admitted, "but we know what to expect if we stay here. Just more of the same nonsense we've been putting up with for the last few months."

"But aren't the whiteshirts leaving?"

"So?" Ms. Chang laughed scornfully. "The yellowshirts will be staying and a yellowshirt is just a whiteshirt of another color." She smiled at Gavven again. "I don't know about you, Gavven Janus, but I like to think for myself. And if that means running off to another world, then I'll run! Everybody here seems to feel the same way."

"Mom and Dad and I just want to keep Sudeshi," Gavven said. "The whiteshirts want to send her away with Jamal Singh and his family to an Indian world."

"Jamal and Indiri," Ms. Chang said thoughtfully. "Indiri is a bright child, but Jamal... Oh well, enough of that. Let's go see what our families are discussing."

Mom and Dad were still talking to Mr. Chang. Sudeshi was bouncing in Mom's arms.

"So, what's going on now?" Ms. Chang asked. "Samm?"

"I've been explaining to Dave and Ruth that we're going to use the random setting feature he and I were working on before he got fired. I have managed to get the program up and running," Mr. Chang said.

Dad nodded. "That's what we had planned to do ourselves, but the problem was getting hold of the generator. Samm seems to have that all wrapped up!"

"He certainly does," Ms. Chang agreed. "Who'd have guessed that my son had the makings of a major-league thief? How he managed to get an entire working generator out of the plant without anyone noticing is beyond me!"

"I didn't steal the generator," Mr. Chang laughed. "I made it."

"Out of components you stole," his mother said with mock severity. "But never mind. Did you tell them when we think we're leaving?"

"Just a few days before the official relocation date," Mr. Chang said. "The whiteshirts will be too busy to take any notice of us, and it will give us time to..."

His voice stopped abruptly.

"What's the matter?" Ms. Chang asked.

"Ssh! Something's happening," Mr. Chang said. He cupped his hand around the earpiece he was wearing and listened. "It's the whiteshirts, Dave," he said in a low voice. "They're searching for the four of you."

"Where are they?" Dad hissed.

"Too close," Mr. Chang replied. "They must have tracked you here somehow... They're outside now and though it'll take them some time to get in, they are bound to find us."

He ran over to an enormous, ancient looking box. He tore through the cardboard and underneath it was an intricate machine. "This is the Glory Gate generator I built," he said. "Help me get it going, Dave."

Dad bent and began keying in commands while Mr. Chang fiddled with some of the dials. The other people in the long chain of attics began to move around uneasily. Gavven watched the different groups. There were all kinds of people, including some mixed families like his own.

"Are we leaving right now?" Ms. Chang asked sharply.

"I hope not," her son said. "But we need to be ready in case we have to escape."

"Then everyone else better be ready, too." Ms. Chang began to pass the word.

Soon everyone was picking up boxes or bundles or crates.

"We're in for it now – they're definitely coming in!" Mr. Chang exclaimed, working even faster.

This is crazy, Gavven thought suddenly. It couldn't really be happening. Surely he'd wake up in a moment, and find himself lying in his own bed, with Sudeshi singing to herself in her crib next door. He would still be best friends with Jamal, and there would be no such thing as a whiteshirt...

There was a loud crackling sound outside in the street, and a persuasive voice began to speak over a bullhorn.

"Davit and Rutha Janus? We know you're in there." The voice chuckled. "Our remote heat sensors prove that Wing Terrace isn't as abandoned as it looks. We believe you are hiding in there with quite a few other people we've been missing. Come out immediately, and we'll take young Sudeshi back to an appropriate family. You have our word that nothing more will be done."

There was a pause, broken only by the whirring sound of the Glory Gate generator.

"Come out now," the whiteshirt said. "You have five minutes."

"Or what?" Dad muttered. "Talk, talk, talk." But Gavven noticed Dad's intensity as he finished typing and started clearing a large space in the middle of the room.

"You have four minutes," the whiteshirt said. "You know it is not our government's policy to punish people, but what you are doing is harmful to the future of humankind. The good of the few can never outweigh the good of the many, so we will force you to give up the little girl if we have to."

"They can't get in here, can they?" Mom asked quickly.

"Of course they can!" Ms. Chang said. "And now they know you're here, they will. This isn't a fortress, Ruth. It's just a place we hoped they'd overlook."

People were starting to panic at the whiteshirts' repeated threats. They lined up, but Dad was keeping them away from the area he had cleared. Gavven noticed that when he looked at that area, it seemed like it was starting to shimmer.

"You have three minutes," the whiteshirt said. "If you don't come out before then, we will flood the room with tear gas. It is harmless, of course, but you will not be able to stay in the room. Come out, Davit. Think of the little girl. Tear gas is very painful for adults, and even worse for children."

Mr. Chang checked the generator. "It's ready! I'm maximizing the field," he said. "I hope this new program of ours works, Dave."

Gavven glanced over his shoulder. There were so many people crammed in the long room beyond the attic. How would they all get through Glory Gate fast enough to escape the tear gas?

Mr. Chang switched control of the generator to a remote he held in his hand. By taking the controls with them, there would be no way the whiteshirts could track them down or follow them.

Almost instantly, Gavven felt a whining shiver inside his head. He shook his head to clear it, but that didn't help. His teeth felt strange, as if they were vibrating. His eyes ached and he put both hands over his ears.

"Two minutes," the whiteshirt said.

Sudeshi and several other small children began to cry. Mom's face had turned pale.

A pinpoint danced in front of Gavven's eyes, glittering darkly. Mr. Chang typed another command on his remote and the pinpoint whirled in space. A web of nothing began to spread out from the pinpoint, and a rainbow halo shimmered on its rim.

"We've reached Nilstate!" Mr. Chang said.

"One minute," the whiteshirt said.

There was a pounding sound on the barricaded door through which they had entered. A white gas started to hiss through a crack under the door. People standing near the door moved away, coughing.

"Come out, Davit and Ruth. We will not warn you again."

Chapter 9
GLORY GATE

"I can't believe this is happening!" someone cried loudly.

"We were supposed to have a few more weeks to prepare," another yelled, looking accusingly at Dad.

"We wouldn't be able to do this at all without him – you should thank your lucky stars he's here! Now, get moving!" Mr. Chang shouted as the gas continued to hiss into the room. "We have to get out of here."

The door behind them burst open. Two whiteshirts marched in. They were wearing gas masks that made them look like monsters.

"In a few more seconds," one of them said, "you won't be able to breathe or see."

"We'll breathe freedom once we're through Glory Gate!" Dad said. "If you try to follow us, you'll have to live by the laws we all set up."

The masked faces turned to the generator and the rainbow web of Nilstate.

"Don't do this to yourselves and your children!" one whiteshirt said uneasily as he started to back away. "Don't doom yourselves to an eternity of war! Wars begin because people are different! You all know that."

"No!" Gavven cried. "Wars begin for lots of reasons! Solving one problem won't solve them all!" Suddenly, he reached out and lifted Sudeshi from his mother's arms. Holding his little sister close, Gavven took three running steps and launched himself into Nilstate.

He had no idea what to expect, but he hadn't thought it would be so quiet. So dark. He didn't feel himself land from his leap, but he didn't fall either. There was no heat or cold. He couldn't even feel the weight of his little sister. He tried to move his hands and feet, but it was is if they weren't there anymore.

We didn't pack anything to help us get started, he thought. I didn't say good-bye to my friends.

There was more silence… more nothing.

What will we eat? Gavven wondered. What if we land in a desert? What if we never land at all?

And then there was a sudden burst of glorious rainbow colors. As the dark exploded into fireworks, Gavven could suddenly feel the weight of Sudeshi in his arms again. Then the ground came rushing to meet his feet. A cool breeze whispered against his face and he tumbled into a patch of sweet-smelling grass, holding tightly to his little sister.

The sky was gold as well as blue. The grass was a shimmery orange color. A large plant next to him was covered with clusters of purple pods.

The Glory Gate hung in the air for a moment, then Mom and Dad fell onto the grass, with Ms. Chang right behind them, clutching a large bag of books and pens.

Paper books! Gavven wondered where she'd found them.

More people spilled through the gate, pale and dark, old and young, wailing with fear or laughing with excitement. Mom and Dad scooped up Gavven and Sudeshi and moved them out of the way as boxes and crates and bundles and bags and cans bounced and fell through Nilstate into the grass.

There was a pause, then Mr. Chang stepped through, and in his hands he held the remote control for the Glory Gate generator.

The rainbow shimmer dimmed.

"That's the end of that," Mr. Chang said as Nilstate vanished. "While the whiteshirts were waiting for reinforcements to arrive, I was able to enter one last program command. After Glory Gate sent me through, I set it to erase all previous commands. Short of checking every random world in the universe, they will never find us."

"Does that mean we can't go back?" someone asked.

Ms. Chang walked over to her son. "Of course we can't go back!" she said. "Who would want to go back? We're all going forward into a new world."

Gavven looked around. There were Mom and Dad, Sudeshi, Ms. Chang, and Mr. Chang. And there, among the other people who had come, he began to see a few familiar faces. Others were strange, but he'd know them soon enough.

There was a silence, and Sudeshi began to struggle in his arms. Dazed, Gavven put her down and watched as she ran toward two other children. They turned to watch her come, a white child and his black brother.

"Hello, friends! Come play, friends!" Sudeshi shouted happily.

From the Author

I always enjoy writing science fiction, and I'm interested in the way people live. Where do the rules come from? Are they always good rules, or not?

In a democratic country we choose our politicians and trust them to make decisions for us. What if they began making rules that changed the ways in which we live our private lives? What if they decided who could live with whom? How would a child feel if a brother or sister were taken away?

These things interest me, but I had never thought of writing a book about them. Then one lovely bright day, as I was out walking,

I found myself wondering what it would be like if all the colors were different, if the sky were yellow and the grass blue, if the glorious sunset were green instead of red.

Suddenly, a title popped into my mind: *Glory Gate*. I started thinking of a story to go with the title. What if there were a gate into another dimension? Would I go through that gate? What would make me go through if I knew I could never come back? My family is very important to me, and if someone told me I could never see my loved ones again, I might go through the gate so we could be together. By the time I was back home at my computer, I had the story ready in my mind.

I enjoyed seeing how Gavven tries to keep his family together. I hope you enjoy this story, and I hope it makes you ask as many questions as it raised for me when I wrote it.

Sally Odgers

DISCUSSION STARTERS

1. In their desire to create a perfect society, the planners of Gavven's community think that segregation will create harmony. What might be the consequences of a segregated society?

2. Gavven carries his sister, Sudeshi, through Glory Gate, but their parents slip through only at the last minute. What challenges would Gavven face if he had to raise his sister on his own?

3. Traveling through Nilstate, with no idea of where he was going, must have been frightening for Gavven. Can you imagine what Nilstate would be like? Try to describe your idea of what lies beyond Glory Gate.